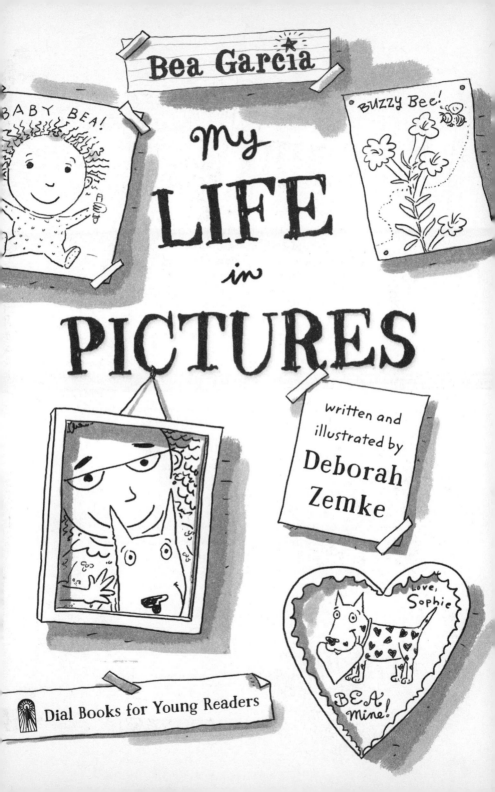

DIAL BOOKS FOR YOUNG READERS
Penguin Young Readers Group
An Imprint of Penguin Random House LLC
375 Hudson Street
New York, New York 10014

Text and illustration copyright © 2016 by Deborah Zemke

Library of Congress Cataloging-in-Publication Data

Zemke, Deborah.
My life in pictures / by Deborah Zemke.
pages cm.—(Bea Garcia)
Summary: When budding artist Bea Garcia's best friend moves to Australia and a loud,
rambunctious boy moves into her old house, Bea must learn to make new friends.
ISBN 978-0-8037-4154-6 (hardcover)
[1. Friendship—Fiction. 2. Drawing—Fiction. 3. Hispanic Americans—Fiction.] I. Title.
PZ7.Z423My 2016   [Fic]—dc23   2014049059

Manufactured in the USA

1 3 5 7 9 10 8 6 4 2

Designed by Mina Chung • Text set in Albertina

To Yvonne,
and all best friends,
then and now

CHAPTER 1:
THIS BOOK IS MY LIFE!

The book you're holding in your hands is my life. I draw pictures of EVERYTHING in it.

I draw pictures of my favorite things.

dancing
elephant

vanilla cake
with red-hot
polka dots

stars to make
wishes on

new
pencil

flowers

Sophie,
my dog

I draw pictures of my not-favorite things.

broken
pencil

my little brother,
the Big Pest!

books
I can't
draw in

monsters

getting up
for school

I draw pictures of what has really truly happened to me. This is when I met my little brother for the first time.

I draw pictures of what I WISH would happen to me, like if I had hundreds of best friends at the same time.

Sometimes I draw pictures of things that could only happen in pictures, like if I could fly around the world.

Or shake hands with an octopus.

This is me. Beatrice Holmes Garcia.

Even though my name is Beatrice, everybody calls me Bea. Except my mom. She calls me Honey Bea.

Except in the morning.

Or when she's mad at me, like the time I turned my little brother into a vampire with Magic Marker.

Or when I drew a herd of elephants dancing on the wall with her lipstick.

My dad liked the picture.

He wasn't so crazy about the mustache
that I drew on the brand-new TV.

I think Wendy the Weather Woman
looks good with a mustache.

This is my little brother, the Big Pest. I think he looks better as a vampire.

We don't look anything alike except maybe around the eyes. His name isn't really truly the Big Pest, even though he is one. His name is Pablo. My mom calls him Pablito.

This is Sophie, the smartest dog in the world.

This is my family. My dad's not in the picture because after I ruined the new TV, he said I couldn't draw him for fifteen years.

So here we are fifteen years from now. My brother is an even bigger pest and I'm a movie star. I WISH!

This is our house. My dad calls it *our little hovel*. I asked him what a hovel was. He said that I should look it up in a dictionary.

My mom calls our house *nuestra casa*. That's Spanish for *our house*. So, just like I said, this is our house. Not *our little hovel*, whatever that means, and I'm not going to look it up.

This is the crabapple tree in our back-yard. It's just the right size for me to climb and too big for a little brother to climb.

Unless something scares that little brother.

Something scares him so much that he runs and jumps into the branches without thinking about how big the tree is.

That's the Big Pest at the top. He got up, but he's too scared to come down.

This is the hero Fireman Dave, who got him down.

And now I'm going to tell you the really true story of the monster who chased him up, with pictures to prove it really truly happened.

CHAPTER 2
MY FIRST AND
ONLY BEST FRIEND

This is my first and only best friend, Yvonne. She is NOT the monster.

On my fifth birthday, just as I was about to blow out the candles on my favorite vanilla cake with red-hot polka dots, the doorbell rang and Yvonne made my birthday wish come true.

It was like magic. We were best friends, and it was my best birthday ever. We ate cake and drew pictures of elephants dancing on the paper tablecloth with my mom's old lipstick.

We made a mustache for the Big Pest and one for my mom, one for my dad, and one for Sophie the dog, too.

This is the Fabulous Palace that we made out of the box Yvonne's new washing machine came in. We put it in Yvonne's front yard. We drew pictures of strange and beautiful flowers on the out-side. We drew pic-tures of elephants and kangaroos on the inside.

We both lost our first tooth at the same time. We went to our first day of kindergarten together and to all of our first days of school after that. We sat together for Story Time and learned our ABCs together, and how to read and write. We counted our Halloween candy together.

I have:
   4 Choco Drops
+ 9 boxes of Hot Dots
+ 10 Twirls
+ 5 Lemon Blasters
+ 5 Peanut Barks
_____
33 treats!

I have:
   11 Choco Drops
+ 7 boxes of Hot Dots
+ 7 Twirls
+ 5 Lemon Blasters
+ 3 Peanut Barks
_____
33 treats!

We played together at recess and after school, on weekends and vacations, running back and forth in the backyards from my house to her house.

One winter day, we rolled a snowball from her yard to mine and back a hundred times until it was the biggest snowball in the world. Then we turned the snowball into a giant Snow Kitty.

I don't think Sophie liked Snow Kitty.

When it was warm, we played in the crabapple tree that was just the right size for us to climb.

It was a magic tree.

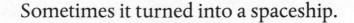

Sometimes it turned into a spaceship.

Sometimes it was the tallest mountain in the world.

Sometimes we swam in the ocean of its branches.

That was before. Before Yvonne moved away and the real monster moved in.

CHAPTER 3

MY FIRST AND ONLY USED-TO-BE-UNTIL-SHE-MOVED-A-MILLION-MILES-AWAY BEST FRIEND.

This is Yvonne and me the night before she moved a million miles away.

Yvonne moved to Australia on my birthday. This time my birthday wish did NOT come true.

The vanilla cake with red-hot polka dots tasted rotten. I gave my piece to Sophie the dog even though I knew the polka dots would make her burp.

I felt rotten. I couldn't draw dancing elephants or make a mustache for my dad.

I felt ROTTEN! I couldn't play in the Fabulous Palace or swim in the ocean of the magic tree. And even though he begged me, I couldn't turn the Big Pest into a vampire.

I FELT ROTTEN! All I could do was think over and over

This is the moving truck that took her stuff away.

This is the car that took her away.

This is the recycling truck that almost took away the Fabulous Palace except Sophie and I rescued it and put it in our front yard.

This is the letter I tried to write, but didn't send because it was too stupid.

Dear Yvonne,
I wish you didn't move away.
I wish you didn't move away.
I wish you didn't move away.
I wish you didn't move away.
I wish you didn't move away.
I wish you didn't move away.

AND I WISH THE MONSTER
DIDN'T MOVE IN!

CHAPTER 4
THE MONSTER NEXT DOOR

After Yvonne moved away, my mom tried to cheer me up. I tried to imagine somebody nicer than Yvonne, but all I could imagine was this black cloud.

My dad tried to make me feel better, too.

So did the Big Pest and Sophie.

*In dog that means, *Here's my best stick just for you.*

My dad even made me his famous BIG chip cookies.

But I wasn't cheered up. I just sat in the backyard and watched the Big Pest throw sticks for Sophie. He threw and threw and she ran in circles looking for the sticks. But she never found any of them.

I felt sorry for her so I drew this picture of Super Sophie.

This is the truck that pulled in next door while Sophie was chasing sticks. It wasn't a moving truck. There wasn't somebody nice my age in it.

There were only these two men who unloaded a wheelbarrow, a shovel, string, sticks, a big bag, and lots of wood.

The Big Pest was pretty excited.

Sophie was excited, too, especially about the sticks.

The men put a stick in each corner of Yvonne's yard and tied string from one stick to the next. They dug twelve holes, stuck a post in each one, and filled them with cement. They were nailing wood to the posts when Mom called us in for lunch.

After lunch, we couldn't see the men anymore. We couldn't see what used to be Yvonne's yard anymore, either.

All we could see was this fence.

This is me scaring the Big Pest.

This is him stuck in the crabapple tree because he was so scared that he jumped up without thinking about how big the tree is and how little he is. He got up, but he's too scared to come down.

Here's our hero, Fireman Dave, who got him down. And now you know that it wasn't a monster who chased the Big Pest up the tree. It was me. The first time.

But it really truly was a monster the second time. Really. Keep reading and I'll prove it to you.

CHAPTER 5

THE REALLY TRULY MONSTER NEXT DOOR

Everybody was so busy watching Fireman Dave rescue the Big Pest that they didn't see the moving truck that came next door.

Everybody except me.

I *was* sorry that I'd scared the Big Pest. It wasn't his fault that Yvonne moved away. He didn't make the fence.

I told the Big Pest that I would turn him into a vampire, but he didn't want to play with me.

He only wanted to throw sticks for Sophie in the backyard. He wouldn't let me play. Even Sophie wouldn't let me play.

I just watched.

Something else watched, too.

Something on the other side of the fence.

Something growly that wasn't a dog.

There goes the Big Pest. Guess where he's running?

Yep, right back up in the crabapple tree.

Fireman Dave got him down again. But this time it wasn't me who scared him up there. It was the monster on the other side of the fence.

My mom was wrong.

CHAPTER 6

MEET YOUR NEW NEIGHBOR

Here's my mom with more of Dad's cookies...

Just as Pablo was about to run out the door and back up into the crabapple tree for the third time, the doorbell rang.

It wasn't somebody nice my age.

It was the monster with his mother.

Bert did look like a monster to me. Doesn't he to you?

He didn't look like a monster to the Big Pest. Not at first.

In fact, Pablo thought it was funny when Bert stuffed five cookies into his mouth.

And burped.

Sophie liked the cookie crumbs that went flying everywhere.

But then Bert scared the Big Pest.

He scared Sophie.

He didn't scare me. He just made me mad. Really mad.

Because he knocked down the Fabulous Palace. And jumped on it. And flattened it. And everybody knew he really was a monster.

Everybody except my mom.

When I turned the no-longer Fabulous Palace into a sign and put it in Bert's front yard, she made me take it down.

I felt ROTTEN. Instead of Yvonne and the Fabulous Palace, there was a monster and a big fence. The magic crabapple tree wasn't magic anymore. I couldn't swim in its branches or climb to the clouds or fly to Saturn.

I could only sit with Sophie, the world's only tree-climbing dog.

Except, thanks to Bert the Monster, she's the world's only tree-climbing-up-but-not-down dog.

*That's dog for *gracias* which is Spanish for *thanks*.

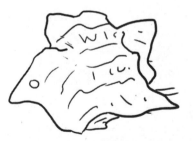

This is the second letter I tried to write to Yvonne in Australia, but didn't send.

What could I say? How could I tell Yvonne that a monster had moved into her house and now there was a big fence between her backyard and mine?

How could I tell her the Fabulous Palace had been flattened and the crabapple tree wasn't magic anymore? The spaceship and ocean and mountain in my backyard were all just pretend make-believe kid stuff.

I couldn't say any of it. I could only write:

I WISH YOU DIDN'T MOVE AWAY!

I WISH YOU DIDN'T MOVE AWAY!

CHAPTER 7
MY WORST FIRST DAY OF SCHOOL EVER

This is me on the first day of school.

I felt rotten because not only was I not going to the first day of school with my best friend, Yvonne, I was going with my little brother, the Big Pest.

And a monster named Bert.

The kind of monster that scares little kids like the Big Pest.

The kind of monster that calls you names.

And then everyone laughs at you.

At least I didn't have to introduce Bert
to my friends, because I had no friends.

But I didn't think my worst first day of
school could get any worse.

Until it did. These are the twenty kids in my new class.

65

Please find the desk with your name and have a seat.

Here are the desks set in five rows across and four rows back.

Here's my name on the desk in the front row next to the windows. That wasn't worse, not at all, because I like sitting by the windows.

This is Judith Einstein, the smartest girl in the universe, whose desk is in the front row right next to mine.

Einstein acts like she has never seen me before in her life even though we have been in the same class since kindergarten.

But I'm still glad she sits next to me because Mrs. Grogan will love to call on her, and the more Mrs. Grogan calls on Einstein, the less she will call on me.

So if Einstein sits right beside me and the windows are on the other side, what could be worse? Guess!

Guess who sits right behind me?

Yes, you guessed it. Bert the Monster sits right behind me. It's not fair!

I WISH Tristan or Keisha could sit behind me. Tristan is nice. Keisha is smart and funny.

But Tristan and Keisha sit way over on the other side of the room. They may as well be on the other side of the world.

I WISH I could take a trip around the world.

I WISH Lauren or Megan or Marcus sat behind me. Or Adelaide or Tommy. Or anybody. Walter could sit behind me. That would be fun.

That's it! Walter the bunny could sit behind me.

74

Then Bert the Monster could sit in Walter's place, way in the back, where he belongs. I WISH!

Here I am, introducing our new class-mate.

This is everybody laughing except Einstein. This is Mrs. Grogan so mad it looked like there was smoke coming out of her ears.

Here I am, NOT introducing our new classmate as the monster he really truly is.

This is the pencil I didn't use to draw a picture of Bert when he really truly stood up and took off his hat.

Because Bert didn't tell his new friends and fellow explorers about himself. He burped. Yes, again! Only this time in school, in front of everybody. Nobody laughed. I don't need to draw a picture.

Mrs. Grogan decided we weren't ready to sail on our ships of discovery. Instead we started our journey together by writing Good Behavior Rules.

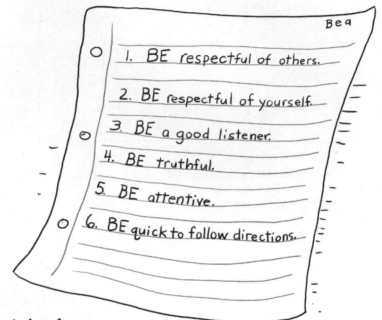

Bea

○ 1. BE respectful of others.

2. BE respectful of yourself.

○ 3. BE a good listener.

4. BE truthful.

5. BE attentive.

○ 6. BE quick to follow directions.

Bees just like you, Bumble Bea.

BE quiet, Bert.

Really, we just needed one rule: *Be NOT a monster.*

CHAPTER 8
THE MOST EXTREME PLACES ON EARTH

This is me on the second day of school.

Here we are walking to the bus stop and yes, I am holding the Big Pest's hand.

It wasn't my idea. But the Big Pest wasn't sure if Bert was really truly a monster so he grabbed my hand and wouldn't let go.

Because he was a little scared, the Big Pest didn't want to sit near Bert on the bus. Instead we sat next to Einstein, who acted like she had never seen me before in her life. I could hardly hear Bert four rows back.

It *was* different. Bert growled and burped. He ruined the Fabulous Palace and the magic tree. Bert ruined everything. He even tried to ruin *My Life*.

Bert did just what I asked. He let go.

I went flying.

I wasn't okay. I was MAD. Really mad.

I'm not going to draw you a picture of how I felt because if I did, I would look like a monster and I am NOT the monster. Bert is! So just imagine me taking the Big Pest to his classroom.

Imagine how I felt in Mrs. Grogan's class, where my ship of discovery was still right in front of Bert's.

Imagine me WISHING I could send Bert flying.

The lowest place on Earth sounds like the perfect spot for Bert!

> Tristan and Keisha, please pass out these Top Ten Geography notebooks. You'll use your notebook to make a record of each place that we visit. Now open your notebooks to page one.

Mrs. Grogan turned out the lights and turned on the projector. Everybody opened their Top Ten Geography notebooks.

Everybody except me. I opened my book, the one you're reading now, *My Life in Pictures*. I turned to a brand-new page.

36,000 feet below sea level? That sounds like a great place for you, Bert! I hope you can swim!

Here's my drawing of Bert where he belongs—in a shark cage 36,000 feet below sea level. Hold your breath, Bert!

Here's Bert, 29,000 feet up at the tip-top of the world. Don't look down, Bert!

It's hot enough to set your hair on fire,
Bert! Wear plenty of sunscreen!

Here's Bert in Antarctica. Don't feed the penguins!

Ha-ha-ha-ha, Bert, you are flying in . . .

No! No! No way! I can't send Bert to Australia!

This is me trying to erase my picture of
Bert in the middle of a cyclone in Australia.

This is everybody else outside at recess.

And me wishing I didn't press so hard on the paper when I draw.

This is Mrs. Grogan with really truly smoke coming out of her ears.

This is me hiding under my desk because Mrs. Grogan is holding *My Life* in her hands.

This is Mrs. Grogan, looking at my pictures of Bert in the cyclone and Bert in Antarctica and Bert in Death Valley and on Mount Everest and way down under the Pacific Ocean.

This is Mrs. Grogan looking at my pictures of Yvonne and me in the magic tree and the Fabulous Palace and the Big Pest and my mom and dad and Wendy the Weather Woman and Fireman Dave. Fireman Dave, if only you could rescue me now.

This is Mrs. Grogan, sending me to the absolute lowest place on Earth.

CHAPTER 9
THE LOWEST PLACE
ON EARTH

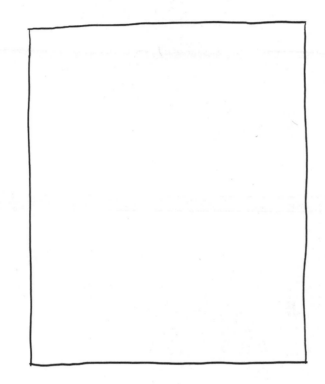

This picture is blank because I am on the playground without my pencil, without my book.

This picture is blank because I don't want to think about what will happen next when recess is over.

CHAPTER 10
THE MONSTER ON
TOP OF THE WORLD

This is really truly what happened next when recess was over.

I looked at Einstein. I looked at Mrs. Grogan. Why didn't she call on Einstein if she wanted the right answer?

I closed my eyes. I could hear Bert behind me breathing. Then I remembered drawing him on . . .

Mount Everest?

That's right. Bea, how high is Mount Everest, the highest place on Earth?

I closed my eyes. I could see Bert on top of Mount Everest. Then I remembered.

29,000 feet?

Yes, it is 29,000 feet above sea level, and there is someone in our class, a Top Ten Explorer, who has been to the top.

You're smart, Bumble Bea.

Be quiet, Bert.

And then Mrs. Grogan turned on the projector and showed the picture.

You know the one.

This one. The picture I drew of Bert on top of Mount Everest.

This is everybody laughing, except me.

This is me hiding under my desk while Mrs. Grogan showed my pictures of Bert on Mount Everest, and Bert in the Pacific Ocean, and Bert in Antarctica and Death Valley, and Bert waving in the wind in Australia.

This is everybody cheering and Bert acting like he really truly was on top of the world.

This is me hiding under my desk, where I will NOT hear everyone laughing when Mrs. Grogan shows all the other pictures in my book, of Yvonne and me and the Fabulous Palace and the Big Pest.

All those pictures of what really truly happened and all those pictures of what I WISH would happen. This is me hiding under my desk at the bottom of the universe, where I will NOT hear everyone laughing at *My Life in Pictures*.

CHAPTER 11
I'M AN AMAZING ARTIST!

ut Mrs. Grogan didn't show any more pictures. She turned off the projector and turned on the lights.

Then she picked up the answer from
my desk and showed it to the class.

Everybody—even Bert—knew the
answer to that question.

I peeked out from the bottom of the universe. I didn't hear anyone laughing.

Here is what I heard.

And like magic, the second day of school got better than I could ever have wished for.

Even recess.

Even lunch.

Even Bert. For the first time, Bert didn't growl, burp, or call me names. He was quiet.

Here is Mrs. Grogan giving me back my book. She gave me back *My Life*.

Here I am sitting with Einstein again on the bus. This time she talked to me.

I think that meant she liked my pictures.

I knew that meant she really liked my pictures.

I didn't walk home from the bus stop with Bert because Trevon and Tommy did.

I did walk home with the Big Pest, which took forever because every few steps he stopped to pick up a stick for Sophie, but that was okay.

Because when I got home, this letter was waiting for me. This letter with the kangaroo stamp. I couldn't have wished for a better second day of school.

CHAPTER 12
MY FIRST LETTER

This is the letter that I got in the mail from Yvonne.

Dear Bea,

I miss you! There are kangaroos and wombats in Australia. It's summer here when it's winter there. Come for a visit! We can go swimming in the Pacific Ocean! Here's a picture I drew of the Pacific Ocean! Even though you are 10,000 miles away, you are my FIRST and ALWAYS ♡ Best Friend!!! ♡

Yvonne

P.S. Say hi to Sophie for me.

Hi Bea!

I'm a big, furry wombat!

This is the first letter that I finally really truly sent to Yvonne.

Dear Yvonne,

I miss you, too! I'm glad that you weren't in Australia on April 10, 1996, because that was the windiest day ever!! I WISH I could visit you! Do you stand upside down on the other side of the world? Do you have a pet kangaroo?

Your FIRST and ALWAYS BEST FRIEND!

Bea

P.S. Sophie says Woof!

Here are the Top Five Things That I WISH Would Happen:

1. The fastest wind on record, 5,000 miles per hour, blows me to Yvonne's house in Australia.

2. Yvonne and I play with her pet kangaroo.

3. Yvonne and I swim in the real Pacific Ocean.

4. Yvonne and I draw pictures of strange and beautiful flowers on a brand-new Fabulous Palace.

5. My mom and dad really truly say I can visit Yvonne in Australia.

I WISH.

This is the second letter that I really truly sent to Yvonne.

Dear Yvonne,
Guess what? My mom and dad said that someday MAYBE I could come to visit you in Australia. I just have to save enough money for a ticket AND be old enough to fly by myself. HOORAY! I painted a picture of Mount Everest on the fence that Bert's family put up between my house and yours.

your 1st and ALWAYS best friend!
Bea

P.S. Bert is the monster who moved into your house.

I really truly did paint a picture of
Mount Everest on the fence.

The Big Pest and Sophie helped.

So did Bert.

I think Bert looks good with a mustache.

This is me, Beatrice Holmes Garcia. This is my book, or I should say, my FIRST book. It's okay if you laughed at my pictures. They're supposed to be funny.

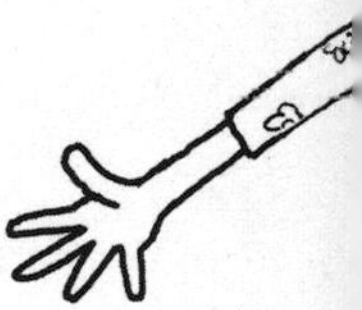
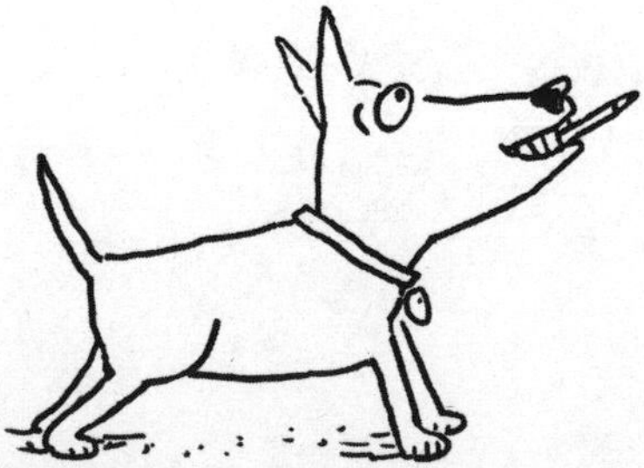

This is the pencil of the
smartest girl in the universe.

It has magical powers.

It will either turn
me into a star.

Or a monster.

Find out in the
second book about
Bea Garcia, Artist

The Curse of

Einstein's Pencil

Coming in 2017